Lettuce Prey

Alex Westhaven

Lettuce Prey
ISBN 978-1-937477-36-3

Published by Brazen Snake Books

Edited by Carol R. Ward

Also by the Author

Sprouted

Jack

Angel Eyes

No Hazard Pay

Lettuce Prey

He was feeding the bitch cake. Off his own fork.

Bastard.

Abby Mars peered through the small portal window in the swinging door that separated the kitchen from the dining room. Her ears burned with anger as she watched her boyfriend with another woman. Not just any woman, but a fat cow three sizes bigger than the unfortunate top she'd managed to stuff herself into. What she'd done to make Dominic fall for her was anyone's guess, but he could have at least had the decency to tell Abby.

Who did he think he was, anyway - bringing his new fling to her restaurant? Did he think she wouldn't notice just because she was a sous chef, and rarely made it out of the kitchen?

She looked down at the flat stomach she worked so hard for, draped in a stark white jacket. She loved food - there wasn't a dish out there she wouldn't try at least once. But she watched her portions, she was on her feet all day, and three times a week she went to the gym. Dominic appreciated it, or so she thought. Watching him feed the fat girl another bite of chocolate cake made her want to grab the nearest knife and slash his cheating throat.

But she wouldn't. Not here, anyway, where anyone could see and hear. She'd bide her time, plan her revenge, and then they'd die together.

She turned away from the window and strode back to her station. Salads were her assignment today - chopping, dicing, mixing, dressing. The knife flew under her fingers, making a satisfying clunk every time it hit the cutting board. Over the next hour, she forced herself to focus on her job rather than her crumbling love life. She told herself there was no point in worrying about it just yet. Plenty of time for that when she was safely back at the apartment, flinging Dominic's things out onto the front lawn. Her lips curved up slightly at the thought. She'd call a locksmith after work and have him meet her at the house. Then she could just relax and lick her wounds in peace.

When her shift was finished and her station cleaned, she made the call and went home, fitting her key into the lock one last time.

It wouldn't turn.

She frowned and checked her watch. The locksmith wasn't due for twenty minutes yet. She tried the key again, rattling the door knob until it swung open, and Dominic stood on the other side, blocking her entrance.

"Abby, we gotta talk," he said, stepping over the threshold and pulling the door closed behind him. "It's over, babe. I know I shoulda told you before, but it was all kinda fast. Lucinda and me, we want to keep this apartment, but it's okay. I talked to the super, and there was one open just down the hall, so we moved all your stuff for ya. He said you can sign the papers whenever. Here's the key. It's 215."

He pulled a key out of his pocket and reached for her hand, pressing it into her palm. Then he turned and went back into their place, shutting the door in her face with a firm click.

Abby stared at the door for a long moment, letting it all sink in. She could hear them moving around inside, talking, laughing, cozy. Silverware clinked against dishes - her dishes, considering Dominic didn't have any of his own. Apparently he'd forgotten most of the stuff they had was actually hers.

Technically.

Finally turning away, she moved slowly down the hall, stopping in front of 215. Slid the key in the lock. Opened the door.

The apartment was empty.

Abby stared at the expanse as pictures began to form in her mind.

She smiled.

* * *

Sunlight filtered through a crack in the drapes the next morning, falling across Abby's face. She rolled away, squeezing her eyes tighter against the intrusion as her head slipped down onto something considerably harder than her pillow.

"Ow," she moaned, opening her eyes and gazed across a wide expanse of cheap carpet as the night before came rushing back into focus.

"Damn Dominic," she muttered, pushing up into a sitting position on the cold floor. Her hand brushed something soft and she grasped her jacket, pulling it on and zipping it tight around her body.

Remembering the sun that so rudely woke her, she got to her feet and went to the window, pulling the drapes open wide so she could soak up the warmth. Leaning against the frame, she thought about the plan she'd decided on last night. She'd tossed and turned on the floor, considering all the ways it could go wrong, and how to keep that from happening. Fairly certain she hadn't missed anything, she'd finally drifted off to sleep. Now in the bright daylight, she mentally ran through the various scenarios again, knowing if she wasn't completely thorough, it would all be for naught.

Half an hour later, she grabbed her purse and keys and went shopping. Five garage sales, three thrift shops and a grocery store later, she parked at the back of her building and hauled her loot up the stairs, reminding herself that it was both good exercise and for a worthy cause. When she was finally done putting away the last of the groceries, she made herself a sandwich and sat on an upside-down plastic milk crate to survey her wares.

The old folding table would be the central focus, covered with a nice tablecloth borrowed from the restaurant, and adorned with two silver-plated candlesticks she'd gotten for a quarter. A dusty silk plant would need to be showered off before serving as a centerpiece.

Rusty folding lawn chairs would be paired with pieces from someone's old mattress pad, and covered with white sheets tied into big poofy bows at the back just like on those fancy home decor shows. A set of old silverware waited to be polished and set out on elegant blue cloth napkins.

Abby glanced over at the kitchen counter and sighed. She really would have liked to keep the transparent blue glass dish set and glassware, but for this to work, everything had to be considered disposable.

Finishing her sandwich, she washed her hands and checked her watch. Her shift started in an hour, but there would be time enough after to get everything set up.

Reaching for a pen, Abby took an elegant purple card with white lilies on the front out of an envelope, and scribbled a short note inside. Slinging her purse over her shoulder, she walked down the hall and taped the card to Dominic's door on her way to the car.

* * *

Tired from her shift at the restaurant, Abby stowed the extras she'd brought home in the refrigerator, and then spent the next several hours putting everything in place. The plastic was a little challenging, but by six the next morning her temporary quarters had been transformed into a fine dining room that was sure to impress. The kitchen was prepared for efficient food preparation, and the other tools she'd need were laid out neatly in one of the bedrooms along with a checklist to ensure nothing was forgotten.

Laying down on a cheap sleeping bag she'd picked up at one of the garage sales she'd stopped at the day before, she set the alarm on her cell phone for six hours and drifted off to sleep with a smile.

Before the alarm could go off, an insistent pounding woke Abby from a deep, restful sleep. She yawned, then frowned as the knocking at her door grew louder and faster. Stumbling to the door, she checked the peephole and sighed. Fortifying herself with one more deep breath in and out, she opened the door just wide enough to slip outside, pulling it shut behind her.

"I'm afraid I don't remember your name," she told Dominic's new girlfriend.

The bitch held up the purple card, shaking it back and forth. "What the hell is this? Are you trying to get him back? Because I'm not going to tolerate this shit. You leave my man alone. Hear that? *My* man!"

Abby shrugged, trying to look bored. "I'm not trying to get him back - you won him fair and square." *Not!* "I just thought it would be nice for us to get to know each other is all, since we're going to be neighbors and all. Did he tell you I'm a sous chef? I wanted to make you both a nice meal. That's all. It could be fun, don't you think?"

The other woman stared at her with narrowed eyes, clearly skeptical. "Why would you want to do anything nice for me? That doesn't make sense. We both like the same guy. That makes us enemies."

"Wanna know a secret?" Abby looked both ways down the hall, as if checking to make sure no one else was around. "I was going to break up with Dominic anyways. I don't love him - haven't for a long time. So you actually did me a favor taking him off my hands." She smiled, nodding her head to accentuate the point as the woman raised her eyebrows, her lips slowly curving upwards.

"Get out," she said, putting her hands on her more-than-ample hips. "Why would you want to break up with my boy? Is there something I should know? You gotta tell me if there is..."

Abby laughed. "No, no. It's nothing like that. I just needed a change, is all. You know, more fish in the sea, and all that." She wiggled her eyebrows, knowing she'd accomplished her goal when the bitch laughed too.

"So, will you come to dinner tonight? You and Dominic, I mean? I've got a really nice menu planned, and it would be a shame for all that nice food to go to waste."

The woman nodded, still chuckling. "We'll be there. Seven, right?"

"That's right." Abby smiled. "I'll see you both then."

* * *

Abby watched Dominic's girl walk down the hall before she went back inside and bolted the door. What had she said her name was?

Didn't matter. Or it wouldn't in a few hours, anyway.

Yawning, Abby checked her watch. It was nearly noon, so no point in laying back down. She retrieved her phone from beside the makeshift bed and rolled up her sleeping bag neatly. Setting it beside the door, she went to the kitchen and began prepping the pork roast for the slow cooker.

As if she'd spend any of her precious time roasting it in an oven for those two. Still, it had to be good and tender, so she mixed a tablespoon of chicken bouillon paste with a can of cherry flavored soda and poured the mixture over the roast in the cooker. Placing the lid on top, she set the cooker to high and then quickly sliced up a head of cabbage, placing it in a smaller slow cooker. Two minced apples and a couple slices of minced bacon went in as well, and a couple tablespoons of apple cider vinegar for good measure. After the glass lid was in place, she turned that pot to low and took off her apron.

Making a quick sweep of the apartment, she placed anything personal in a large tote. Retrieving her keys and purse, she took the tote and the sleeping bag to her car.

The next part would be tricky. Counting the cash from an envelope hidden under her car seat, she drove to a college campus across town and parked. Finding a bench on what seemed like a main pathway between the buildings, she watched students for what seemed like hours until the perfect male finally came into view.

Ordinary, not too intelligent-looking but not stupid either, he was alone and dressed casually in jeans and a t-shirt. The long hair falling across his Buddy Holly glasses seemed to be a shield of sorts, and the old olive military jacket an heirloom, perhaps.

She stood and approached him, her smile friendly as he came closer.

"I was wondering if you could help me," she said in her best damsel-in-distress voice. "There's this guy who has a truck I want, and he won't sell it to me because I'm female. I was wondering if you'd take my money and go buy the truck for me. I'll pay you a fee, of course. How does twenty dollars sound?"

The kid frowned. "How do you know I won't just take your money and run? And why don't you come with me? We'll teach the guy a lesson."

"Oh no," she said, demurely looking away. "I don't want any trouble. I just want the truck. And you look like an honest person. I'd be watching the whole time around the corner." She looked up again, giving him a coy smile and batting her eyes a few times for good measure.

"Pretty please?"

The guy shrugged. "Okay, I guess. Where is this truck?"

"Just a couple blocks that way." She pointed the opposite direction of her car. "We can walk. I really appreciate this."

Fifteen minutes later, she handed the young man a twenty, and he handed her the keys. As she watched him walk back to campus, she almost felt bad for what she'd done, but even if the police harassed him, nothing would come of it. And it would buy her a little time. She fired up the engine and drove back to her temporary apartment, parking in one of the guest spots that was conveniently just outside the door.

It wouldn't be long now. Abby whistled as she made her way upstairs.

* * *

Abby tossed her apron in a garbage bag under the sink as someone knocked on the door. She checked her watch.

"Right on time," she murmured as she went to let them in. Swinging the door wide, she smiled.

"Welcome, you two! I'm glad you came. Have a seat right over there. I'll get drinks." She scurried into the kitchen and checked to make sure everything was in order. Filling the stemware with a light champagne, she carried the flutes to the table.

"Thanks for having us, Abby. Damn decent of you," Dominic said, the woman at his side nodding.

"You're both welcome. It's the neighborly thing to do, don't you think?" She waited for both of them to nod, and then picked up her glass.

"I propose a toast," she said, holding the champagne high. Dominic and the bitch did the same. "To unhappy endings that bring much happiness."

Her guests looked at each other briefly, then shrugged. "To unhappy endings," Dominic repeated, taking a sip, the girl mimicking him.

Abby took a sip as well, and then set her glass on the table.

"I have a lovely pork roast for you tonight, along with some cider cooked cabbage and a fabulous salad. Apple pie for dessert! Now..." she glanced back to the kitchen and decided that instead of making the decision for them as she'd planned, she'd let them do it. It was the least she could do.

Really.

"What should we start with? The main course or the salad?"

"A salad sounds nice," the other woman said. "What kind of dressing do you have?"

Abby grinned and shook her head. "Sorry. It's a secret recipe from the restaurant. But it's very popular. To die for, you might say."

The woman laughed, and Dominic chuckled. "Alright then," he said. "Bring on the death salad."

"As you wish!" Abby went back to the kitchen and plated up three servings from the large stainless steel bowl on ice. Another thing she would've liked to keep. Pity.

Swirling the dressing in a small carafe, she drizzled it over the crisp green leaves and then garnished each plate with a couple thin red onion slices, five croutons and two sliced beet rounds. Taking one plate in hand, she placed another on her forearm and picked up the third to carry them to the table. Taking the third chair, she shook out her napkin and placed it neatly in her lap.

"You'll have to let me know how it is," she said, picking up her fork. "We're not allowed to take written recipes out of the kitchen, so I had to make it from memory." She speared one of the succulent beets, raising it to her lips.

"Wait!"

Abby frowned at the bitch, quickly going over her mental checklist to make sure she hadn't made any mistakes.

"What's wrong, babe?" Dominic set his fork down.

His girl shook her head. "We didn't pray. We should pray over the meal." She seemed to be waiting for a response, and Abby struggled not to laugh. Clearly they hadn't gotten around to discussing Dominic's disdain for all things religion.

Setting her beet down, careful not to let it touch the dressing, Abby sat back in her chair to watch the fireworks.

Dominic stared back for a long moment, the tension almost tangible. Then to Abby's surprise, he nodded once, and held both his hands out, one to each of them.

"Okay babe. If that's what you want."

Wow.

Abby dutifully clasped hands with her guests, bowing her head as the other woman prayed that God would bless the food and gave thanks for such a gracious and understanding neighbor.

"Amen."

Abby smiled and picked up her fork again. "I'm so glad you both came over," she said as her guests each took a bite of salad. "It's good we can spend this time together." Slipping the beet between her lips, she savored the taste and chewed slowly, reaching for the second slice as she watched Dominic's face.

It shouldn't be long now.

"This salad is great," the other woman said, finishing a second bite. "The dressing is tangy - what is that flavor?" Another forkful went into her mouth as Dominic began to choke.

Abby shrugged with a grin. "Just a little secret ingredient. I'm not allowed to tell exactly, but it really adds something special, don't you think?"

The woman's eyes grew wide, and she grasped her throat, letting the fork drop as she reached toward the water glass. Abby set her fork down and dabbed delicately at the corners of her mouth, turning to watch as Dominic convulsed in his chair.

"Quite a punch, I'd say," Abby murmured. Dominic's convulsions stopped, and she turned to the woman, watching until she collapsed against the chair back as well.

Rising to her feet, Abby went to the kitchen and dished up a portion of pork and cabbage from the slow cookers, standing at the counter to eat. She'd rather just get on with the clean up, but the poison needed time to finish the job, and she couldn't very well haul bodies - even properly wrapped - out to her truck until the majority of people would be asleep. It wouldn't pay to hurry. Any little detail could ruin the whole thing.

When she finished her dinner, she snapped on a pair of latex gloves and carefully cleaned up all of the food and dishes, the food down the drain, and the dishes in doubled trash bags. Changing gloves, she checked for a pulse on her guests, satisfied when both wrist and neck gave no indication of life.

Retrieving her tools from the back room, she laid them out on the living room floor and pulled Dominic's body off the chair. Cutting off his clothing, she piled it into a plastic bag and put it by the door. It was time to suit up.

An old hazmat type suit she'd found at one of the thrift stores went on easily over her clothes, taped at the wrists and ankles for extra protection. The gloves were thick, but fit tight enough to allow her to wield the knife and saw easily. Wishing she'd thought to drain the blood while his heart was still beating, she checked the plastic under the fabric on the floor, and got to work.

It took longer than she'd expected to cut him apart.

By the time she finished with both of them, she was exhausted. Her muscles ached, her clothes were damp from sweating inside the suit, and far more bags than she'd thought she'd need were waiting by the door. The floor covering was bright red, and she noted some matching speckles on the wall several feet away.

Damn it.

With a heavy sigh, she looked around and tried to decide how to proceed.

* * *

After spending the next several hours cleaning the apartment, Abby wasn't sure how she could possibly go on any longer. She didn't dare stop though. It wouldn't be long before people started looking for Dominic and what's-her-name, and it would be best if Abby was long gone before that happened.

Downing an energy drink and hoping for a few more hours of darkness, she moved the pickup to a parking spot right near the stairs and started hauling out the trash. She quit counting trips when she reached fifteen, and by the time the first rays of sunlight were breaking over the horizon, she'd just given the apartment one last inspection and locked the door for good.

As she dragged her tired ass down the stairs one last time, a man in too-short shorts, a tight t-shirt and running shoes came out of another apartment. He eyed the truck, then her, smiling sympathetically.

"Moving out?"

She nodded. "Yep. Sucks, but my new place is a lot nicer."

"Good luck with it," he said, moving to go around her. His smile faded as he stared at one of the boxes. "Is that blood?"

Abby glanced over at the offending box, pushing down her sudden panic and forcing herself to breathe.

"Shit," she said, making a show of going over and poking a finger around the damp, dark red cardboard. "I had some meat left in the fridge, and I was hoping it would be okay in the box for just a little while. I'd better go - hopefully I can get to the new place in time to save it."

"I'll let you go then," the man said, a doubtful look on his face. "Drive safe." He jogged down the sidewalk and Abby walked quickly but calmly to the cab of the truck and got in. Turning the key, she started the engine and pulled out of the lot. One of the bags must have broken inside that box, and she wasn't sure what to do other than stick to the plan.

It took twenty minutes to reach her destination, and when she pulled up to the old dry well the thought of moving all those boxes and bags one more inch was more than she could stand. Still, it had to be done, so she backed the truck up as close as she could get. Lowering the tailgate, she dragged, pushed and maneuvered every last bag and box into the stone orifice, listening as they hit the bottom hard. Then she opened the bottles of cleaning solution and poured them in, cringing as a heady chemical smell wafting back up into her face. Closing the tailgate, she moved the truck ten feet away and then got the firecrackers she'd stowed in the glove box.

They'd be louder than she wanted, but it had been the only easy solution to lighting the fire. Flicking a lighter, she lit three fuses and tossed the whole handful into the well. Flinching at the noise, she waited for the popping to stop, and then peered carefully over the edge. Flames grew slowly, as she'd known they would. There wasn't much air down there. If she was lucky, it would burn enough to obscure any real clues. There wasn't anything else she could do.

Getting back in the truck, she drove to the top of a nearby cliff overlooking a deep, narrow valley. Leaving the engine running she got out and reached in to shift it into gear, quickly moving back as it lumbered over the edge. The vehicle crashed hard, bounced, and then landed on it's side before it exploded into a ball of flames.

Abby smiled wearily. All that was left was to hike back to the road and catch a ride to the nearest town. She had enough money to rent a small place while she found a job, and buy a fake social security number to start over as someone new.

Breathing in the fresh morning air, she took a moment to look around, admiring the wild beauty before she had to go. Maybe she'd find a meadow to nap in before she went back to civilization. She didn't really have a deadline any longer.

She'd prepared a small bag to carry her money, a few snacks and several bottles of water. Reaching in, she took out a bottle and unscrewed the cap. Tipping her head back, she took a long drink and then automatically stuck her middle finger in her mouth to lick off excess moisture from the bottle.

She froze for a moment when a sweet, creamy flavor registered on her tongue. Lowering the bottle she examined it closely, noting the errant smear of dressing along one side. Tears prickled in her eyes as she let the cool plastic slip from her fingers. She'd been so careful, hadn't even mixed up the dressing until just before dinner. How could this have happened?

It wasn't long before the convulsions started.

###

About the Author

Alex Westhaven resides in Billings, Montana with her husband and two over-sized lap dogs. Halloween is her favorite holiday, and she has more than her fair share of skeletons (and other body parts) in the closet. Stop by AlexWesthaven.com for all the latest horror news and upcoming books.

www.ingramcontent.com/pod-product-compliance
Lightning Source LLC
LaVergne TN
LVHW041110090826
845145LV00004BA/1467

* 9 7 8 1 9 3 7 4 7 7 3 6 3 *